May this
book bring joy
to your heart!
Linda L. Lee

Nonnie, What's God?

Written by
Linda L. Lile

Illustrated by
Jenniffer Julich

A-Lu Publishing
Traverse City, Michigan

Published by A-Lu Publishing
Traverse City, Michigan

Publisher's Cataloging-in-Publication Data

Lile, Linda L.

Nonnie, What's God? / by Linda L. Lile. – Traverse City, Mich.: A-Lu Pub., 2008.

p. ; cm.

Summary: Grandmother Nonnie shares the most precious love of her life with her granddaughter Abby.

ISBN: 978-0-9817092-0-8

1. God—Juvenile fiction. I. Title.

PZ7 .L56 2008
(E)-dc22   2008926064

Project coordination by Jenkins Group, Inc
www.BookPublishing.com
Illustrations by Jenniffer Julich
Layout by Eric Tufford

Printed in Singapore
12 11 10 09 08 • 5 4 3 2 1

Dedicated to
God, who makes all things possible;
Glen, the love of my life, for support and belief in me;
my son, Jason, and daughters, Tamela and Kimberly;
grandsons, Austin and Parker; and
granddaughter, Abaigael, for her inspiration.

• •

This is a story about Grandmother Nonnie's answers to three-year-old Abby's question.

Nonnie wonders how to tell her granddaughter about the most wonderful "Spirit of Life," Father of Fathers," and "Lord of Lords." After all, Nonnie includes God in every part of her life. Every day begins and ends with her Heavenly Father!

How does a grandmother share this gift with the most precious love of her life?

God gave us grandchildren to love and guide throughout our lives. How do we as grandparents give those children back to Him? We do this by guiding them into His hands.

Every Friday afternoon
I pick up my granddaughter at
daycare.

It has always been exciting for
Abby to be picked up by her
Nonnie. Even at three years
old, Abby couldn't wait for me
to get there!

As I pulled into the driveway,
I could see Abby waiting with
her little face pressed against
the window.

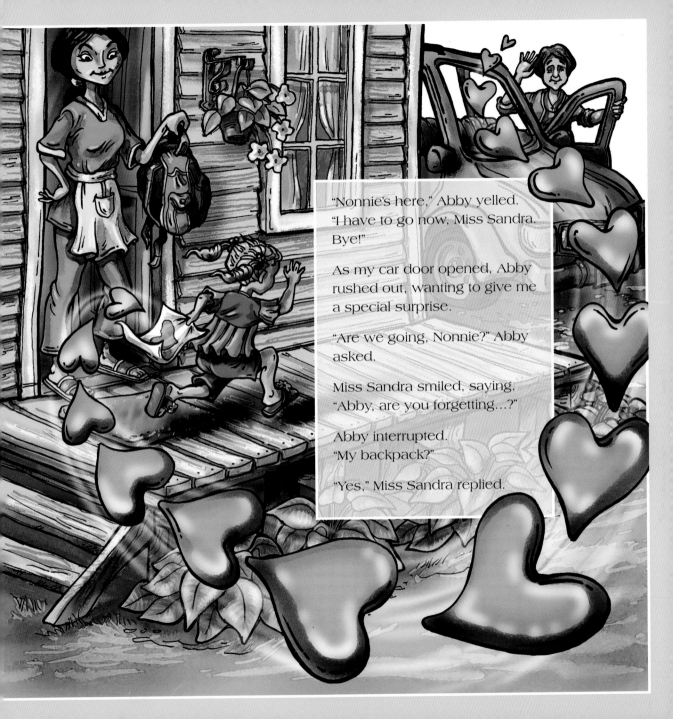

"Nonnie's here," Abby yelled. "I have to go now, Miss Sandra. Bye!"

As my car door opened, Abby rushed out, wanting to give me a special surprise.

"Are we going, Nonnie?" Abby asked.

Miss Sandra smiled, saying, "Abby, are you forgetting...?"

Abby interrupted. "My backpack?"

"Yes," Miss Sandra replied.

"Excuse me, Miss Sandra," "Did she have a good day today?" I asked.

"Come on, Nonnie, let's go!" cried Abby.

I questioned "Are you remembering your manners and being a good listener, Abby?"

"Sorry, Nonnie," apologized Abby.

Miss Sandra smiled again and said, "We're working on her manners, and she did have a great day!"

I thanked Miss Sandra, and said goodbye.

I put Abby into her car seat, as she started to share about her day. She continued talking excitedly as I drove down the street. Abby talked about all her friends at daycare and how they got to play outside. They played games in the morning and had spaghetti and pudding for lunch.

Abby really enjoyed going to Miss Sandra's house.

"Nonnie, I'm hungry," cried Abby.

"When we get home, I will fix you a snack," I said.

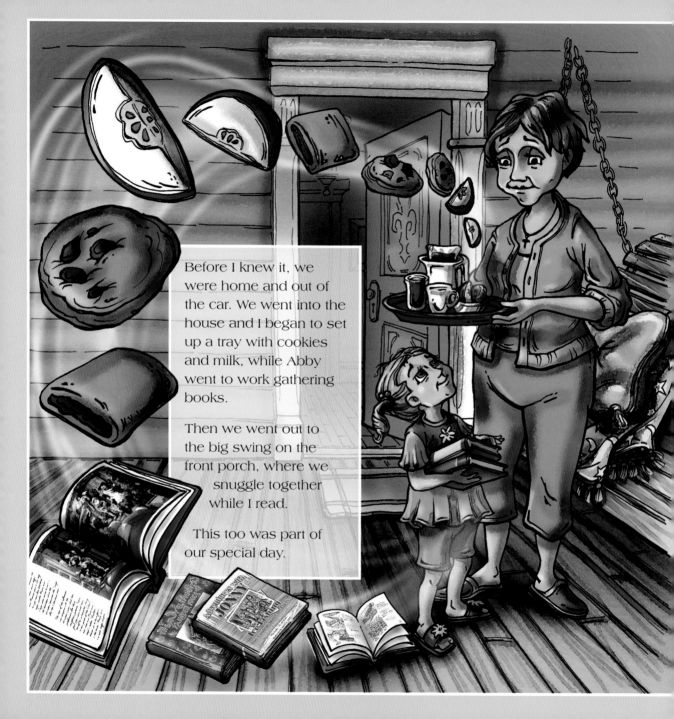

Before I knew it, we were home and out of the car. We went into the house and I began to set up a tray with cookies and milk, while Abby went to work gathering books.

Then we went out to the big swing on the front porch, where we snuggle together while I read.

This too was part of our special day.

I was about to take the first bite of my cookie when it happened.

Abby asked, "Nonnie, what's God?"

Wow! I thought, how do I answer this question? Whatever I say will stay with Abby forever.

How do I explain that God is the Creator of all things? Or how my heart is filled with his Spirit each and every day?

I stopped for a moment, folded my hands to pray and ask Our Heavenly Father to guide my answer, noticing that Abby had done the same.

We cuddled closely together as I began to say,

"The sky is a beautiful blue today. The clouds are fluffy and white. That's from God!

"When the clouds turn gray and the raindrops fall from the sky, when thunder rumbles and the lightning flashes, that's from God!

"When you're sad and all alone, but suddenly your heart feels warm and just wants to sing, that's from God!

"When the sunshine feels warm on your face, and you see a pretty yellow butterfly. That's from God!

"When you scrape your elbow falling, and we cuddle while Nonnie says, 'I love you,' that's from God!

"When Nonnie sees a twinkle in your eye because you're excited that you've seen a puppy for the first time, that's from God!

"When we put our hands together to pray, 'Now I lay me down to sleep,' and Nonnie tucks you in and kisses you goodnight, that's from God!

"When we see the stars in heaven shining through the dark, while the moon shines on your cheek as you are falling to sleep, Nonnie's heart knows that's from God!

"Because Abby, God is Love!"

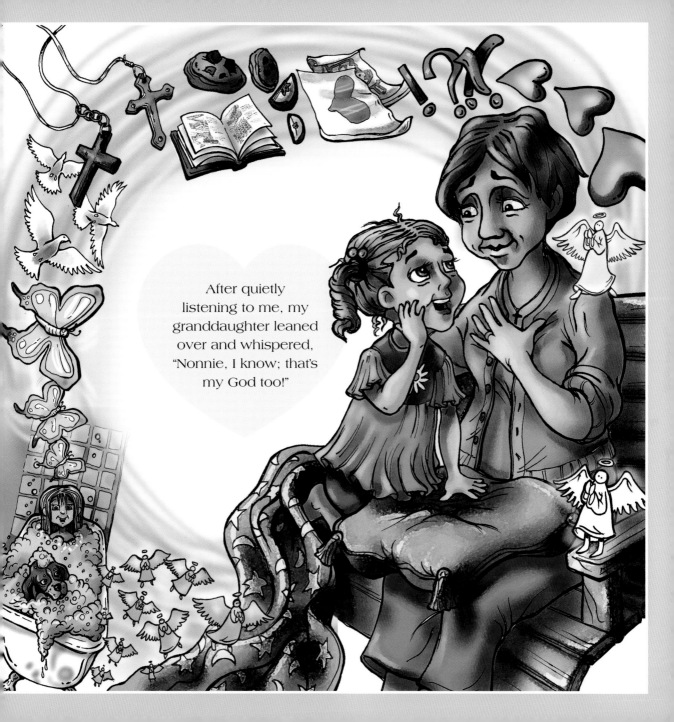

After quietly listening to me, my granddaughter leaned over and whispered, "Nonnie, I know; that's my God too!"

This story was inspired by God. The title is a question my granddaughter actually asked me.

During a spiritual fast and prayers to learn how to be a testimony to my grandchildren, these words came to me at such speed it was hard to get them on paper.

I thank God for this experience, and give him the praise and glory of these blessings.

He that loveth not knoweth not God; for God is love. 1 John 4:8